The Unbreakable Code

by Sara Hoagland Hunter   *illustrated by* Julia Miner

rising moon

For Heather Anne Wilson, who first brought the story of the code talkers to my attention. Her life, like the lives of the code talkers, was an expression of joy in the face of challenge. Her devotion to friends, family, and her Native American heritage inspired the writing of this book.

Special thanks to Carl Gorman and Dean Wilson, two of the original twenty-nine designers of the unbreakable code along with fellow code talkers: Thomas Begay, the late Harold Foster, John Goodluck, John Kinsel, George Kirk, Roy Notha, and their delightful families.—S. H.

For my father, who served in the Pacific, and for all who have laid down their lives for others.

Thank you, Navajo models Jeremy, Daniel, Nissa, and Jeremiah, and your parents. Thanks to the Marine Corps Museum. And a special thank you to the code talkers we interviewed. There never was an actual model for the Grandfather; his character is inspired by all of you. I am in awe of what I have seen of your sacred land and the Navajo Way. Your story, however, transcends time and place and I am grateful for its instruction. —J.M.

www.risingmoonbooks.com

The illustrations in this book were rendered in oil paints on canvas.
The display type was set in Celestia Antiqua/the text type was set in Fournier
Manufactured in China
Production supervised by Lisa Brownfield
Art direction by Trina Stahl and Patrick O'Dell
Designed by Patrick O'Dell and Mary Wages
Edited by Erin Murphy and Katy Spining

FIRST IMPRESSION 1996
ISBN 13: 978-0-87538-917-8
ISBN 10: 0-87358-917-3

Library of Congress Cataloging-in-Publication Data
Hunter, Sara Hoagland.
The unbreakable code / by Sara Hoagland Hunter ; illustrated by Julia Miner.
p.   cm.
Summary: Because John is afraid to leave the Navajo Reservation, his grandfather explains to him how the
Navajo language, faith, and ingenuity helped win World War II.
ISBN 0-87358-638-7
[1. Navajo language—Fiction. 2. Ciphers—Fiction. 3. Navajo Indians—Fiction. 4. Indians of North America—Fiction.
5. Grandfathers—Fiction. 6. World War, 1939-1945—Fiction.] I. Miner, Julia, ill. II. Title.
PZ7.H9185Un 1996
[Fic]—dc20   95-26589

Date of Manufacture : March 2011
Manufactured by : Shenzhen Wing King Tong Paper Products Co Ltd.
Shenzhen, Guangdong, China
Cohort : Batch 1

A Note from the Author

"My shichei (grandfather) was a Navajo code talker. These men are living legends. Kids should know how they helped win the war and how much pain they went through. My shichei always has a smile on his face and a joke ready. I would like to say to him, Thank you for helping win the war for us and for keeping the Navajo tradition alive. Thank you for teaching me so many things."

—MICHAEL GORMAN, age 11

On December 7, 1941, two years after the start of World War II, the Japanese attacked Pearl Harbor in Honolulu, Hawaii. President Franklin Roosevelt immediately declared war on the Axis powers—Japan, Germany, and Italy—marking the entrance of the United States into the war. In the days that followed the bombing, Americans from all walks of life enlisted in the Armed Forces to defend the United States, to fight the rapid expansion of the Japanese Empire, and to join with the Allied Forces to free Western Europe from Germany's control. Among these were a large number of Native Americans. By the end of World War II, 25,000 Native Americans had served. Approximately 3,000 of these were Navajo, including the 420 code talkers who served in the Marine Corps. The code talkers fought on the Pacific islands of Guadalcanal, Bougainville, Tarawa, New Britain, Kwajalein, Roi-Namur, Enewetak Atoll, Saipan, Tinian, Guam, Peleliu, Iwo Jima, and Okinawa. Their contribution of a rapid, unbreakable code saved countless American lives.

It has been a supreme privilege to interview these code talkers and to base a book on their experiences. Their example of modesty, kindness, and strength continues to instruct me.

In honor of the distinguished code talker who asked if I could express his feelings without identifying his name, I offer this conclusion:

Last summer you returned to Saipan. Where fifty years ago you looked out and saw man's desecration of nature, you could now see lush greenery. Where once you had said to yourself in the midnight hour, "Let this never happen to a beautiful island again," you could now announce to an applauding crowd, "You have rebuilt a jewel in the Pacific."

John raced up the trail, sending pebbles skidding behind him. When he reached his favorite hiding place, he fell to the ground out of breath. Here between the old piñon tree and the towering walls of the canyon, he felt safe. The river full of late-summer rain looked like a silver thread winding through his grandfather's farm land. They would be looking for him now, but he was never coming down.

His mother had married the man from Minnesota. There was nothing he could do about that. But he was not going with them. He closed his eyes and rested in the stillness. The faint bleat of a mountain goat echoed off the canyon walls.

Suddenly a voice boomed above him: "Shouldn't you be packing?"

John's eyes flew open. It was his grandfather on horseback.

"Your stepfather's coming with the pickup in an hour."

"I'm not going," John said.

"You have to go. School's starting soon," said Grandfather, stepping down from his horse. "You'll be back next summer."

John dug his toe deeper into the dirt. "I want to stay with you," he said.

Grandfather's soft, brown eyes disappeared in the wrinkles of a smile. John thought they were the kindest eyes he had ever seen.

"You're going to be all right," Grandfather said. "You have an unbreakable code."

"What's that?" asked John.

Grandfather sat down and began to speak gently in Navajo. The sounds wove up and down, in and out, as warm and familiar as the patterns of one of Grandmother's Navajo blankets. John leaned his head against his grandfather's knee.

"The unbreakable code is what saved my life in World War II," he said. "It's the Navajo language."

John's shoulders sagged. Navajo couldn't help him. Nobody in his new school spoke Navajo.

"I'll probably forget how to speak Navajo," he whispered.

"Navajo is your language," said his grandfather sternly. "Navajo you must never forget."

The lump in John's throat was close to a sob. "You don't know what it's like there!" he said.

His grandfather continued quietly in Navajo. "I had to go to a government boarding school when I was five. It was the law.

"They gave me an English name and cut my hair off. I wasn't allowed to speak my language. Anyone who spoke Navajo had to chew on squares of soap. Believe me, I chewed a lot of soap during those years. 'Speak English,' they said. But Navajo was my language and Navajo I would never forget.

"Every summer I went home to herd the sheep and help with the crops. I cried when the cottonwoods turned gold and it was time to go back. Finally, one night in the tenth grade, I was working in the kitchen when I heard a bulletin on the school radio:

"'Navajos needed for special duty to the Marines. Must be between the ages of seventeen and thirty-two, fluent in English and Navajo, and in excellent physical condition.'

"Just before lights out, I snuck past the bunks and out the door towards the open plain. I felt like a wild horse with the lasso finally off its neck. Out in the open, the stars danced above me and the tumbleweeds blew by my feet as I ran. The next day, I enlisted."

"But you weren't seventeen," said John.

"The reservation had no birth records," Grandfather said with a grin. "Two weeks later I was on a bus headed for boot camp with twenty-eight other Navajos. I stared out the window into the darkness. I was going outside of the Four Sacred Mountains for the first time in my life."

"Were you scared?" asked John.

"Of course," said his grandfather. "I didn't know where I was going or what our special mission was. Most of all, I didn't know how I would measure up to the people out there I had heard so much about."

"How did you?" asked John, chewing his fingernail.

His grandfather began to laugh. "We were known as the toughest platoon at boot camp. We had done so much marching at boarding school that the drills were no problem. Hiking in the desert of California with a heavy pack was no worse than hauling water in the canyon in midsummer. And I'd done that since I was four years old.

"As for the survival exercises, we had all gone without food for a few days. A Navajo learns to survive.

"One weekend they bused us to a new camp in San Diego. On Monday we were marched to a building with bars on every window. They locked us in a classroom at the end of a long, narrow corridor. An officer told us our mission was top secret. We would not even be allowed to tell our families. We were desperately needed for a successful invasion of the Pacific Islands. So far the Japanese had been able to intercept and decode all American radio messages in only minutes. This meant that no information could be passed between American ships, planes, and land forces.

"The government thought the Navajo language might be the secret weapon. Only a few outsiders had ever learned it. Most importantly, the language had never been written down, so there was no alphabet for the Japanese to discover and decode.

"He gave us a list of more than two hundred military terms to code. Everything had to be memorized. No trace of the code could ever be found in writing. It would live or die with us in battle.

"When the officer walked out of the room, I looked at the Navajo next to me and began to laugh. 'All those years they told us to forget Navajo, and now the government needs it to save the country!'

"We were marched every day to that classroom. We were never allowed to leave the building. We couldn't even use the bathroom by ourselves. Each night, an officer locked our notes in a safe.

"The code had to be simple and fast. We would have only one chance to send each message. After that, the Japanese would be tracing our location to bomb us or trying to record the code.

"We chose words from nature that would be easy to remember under fire. Since Navajo has no alphabet, we made up our own.

"'A' became *wollachee*."

"Ant?" asked John in English.

Grandfather nodded.

"'B' was *shush*."

"Bear," said John.

"'C' was *moasi*. 'D', *be*. 'E', *dʒeh*." His grandfather continued through the alphabet. Each time he named the Navajo word, John answered with the English.

"We named the aircraft after birds. The dive-bomber was a chicken hawk. The observation plane was an owl. A patrol plane was a crow. Bomber was buzzard.

"At night we would lie in our bunks and test each other. Pretty soon I was dreaming in code.

"Since we would be radiomen, we had to learn all kinds of radio operations. We were taught how to take a radio apart and put it together blindfolded. The Japanese fought at night, so we would have to do most of our work in complete darkness. Even the tiniest match flame could be a target.

"When the day came for the code to be tested in front of the top Marine officers, I was terrified. I knelt at one end of a field with our radio ground set. The officers marched towards me. Behind a building at the other end of the field, another code talker sat under military guard waiting for my transmission. One officer handed me a written message:

"'Receiving steady machine gun fire. Request reinforcements.'

"It took only seconds for me to speak into the microphone in Navajo code. The officer sent a runner to the end of

the field to check the
speed and accuracy of
the message. The Navajo
at the other end handed him
the exact message written in
English before he even came
around the corner of the
building! They tested us over
and over. Each time, we were
successful. The government requested
two hundred Navajo recruits immediately.
Two of our group stayed behind to train
them. The rest of us were on our way."

"Tell me about the fighting!" said John.

Suddenly Grandfather's face looked as creased
and battered as the canyon walls behind him. After a long pause
he said, "What I saw is better left back there. I would not want to
touch my home or my family with those pictures.

"Before we invaded, I looked out at that island. It had been flattened and burned. 'Let this never happen to a beautiful island again,' I thought. I just stayed on the deck of the ship thinking about the ceremonies they were doing for me at home. We invaded at dawn.

"I almost drowned in a bomb crater before I even got to shore. I was trying to run through the water and the bullets when I felt myself sinking into a bottomless hole. My eighty-pound radio pack pulled me straight down. I lost my rifle paddling to the surface.

"On the beach, it was all I could do just to survive. I remember lying there with gunfire flying past my ears. A creek that ran to the beach was clear when I first lay there. By noon it was blood red.

"The worst were the fallen soldiers I had to run over to go forward. I couldn't even stop to say I was sorry. I just had to run over them and keep going.

"I had to move through the jungle at night, broadcasting in code from different locations. One unit needed medical supplies. Another needed machine-gun support. I had just begun broadcasting to another code talker. 'Arizona! New Mexico!' I called. The next thing I knew, an American soldier behind me was yelling, 'Do you know what we do to spies?'

"'Don't shoot!' I said. 'I'm American. Look at my uniform.' He didn't believe me. He had heard the foreign language. He had seen my hair and eyes. Japanese spies had been known to steal uniforms from fallen American soldiers.

"One of my buddies jumped out of the bushes right at that moment and saved my life."

"How did you stay alive the rest of the time?" asked John.

"My belief was my shield," Grandfather answered.

He drew a ragged wallet from deep inside of his shirt pocket. "Inside of this, I carried corn pollen from the medicine man. 'Never be afraid,' he said. 'Nothing's going to touch you.' And nothing ever did. More than four hundred code talkers fought in some of the bloodiest battles of World War II. All but a few of us survived.

"The Japanese never did crack the code. When they finally discovered what language it was, they captured and tortured one poor Navajo. He wasn't a code talker and couldn't understand the message they had intercepted. He told them we were talking about what we ate for breakfast. Our code word for bombs was 'eggs'.

"Six months before the war ended, Navajo code talkers passed more than eight hundred messages in two days during the invasion of Iwo Jima.

"When the American flag was raised on top of Iwo Jima's mountain, the victory was announced in code to the American fleet. 'Sheep-Uncle-Ram-Ice-Bear-Ant-Cat-Horse-Itch' came the code."

John tried to spell out the letters.

"Suribachi?" asked John.

"Yes," said Grandfather. "Mount Suribachi.

"When I came home, I walked the twelve miles from the bus station to this spot. There weren't any parades or parties.

"I knew I wasn't allowed to tell anyone about the code. I looked down at that beautiful canyon floor and thought, 'I'm never leaving again.'"

"But why did you leave in the first place?" asked John.

His grandfather lifted him gently onto the horse. "The answer to that is in the code," he said. "The code name for America was 'Our Mother.' You fight for what you love. You fight for what is yours."

He swung his leg behind John and reached around him to hold the reins. "Keep my wallet," he said. "It will remind you of the unbreakable code that once saved your country."

John clutched the wallet with one hand and held the horse's mane with the other. He wasn't as scared of going to a new place any more. His grandfather had taught him who he was and what he would always have with him. He was the grandson of a Navajo code talker and he had a language that had once helped save his country.

The Original Code

Letter	Navajo Pronunciation	English Word
A	Wol-la-chee	Ant
B	Shush	Bear
C	Moasi	Cat
D	Be	Deer
E	Dzeh	Elk
F	Ma-e	Fox
G	Klizzie	Goat
H	Lin	Horse
I	Tkin	Ice
J	Tkele-cho-gi	Jackass
K	Klizzie-yazzie	Kid
L	Dibeh-yazzie	Lamb
M	Na-as-tsosi	Mouse
N	Nesh-chee	Nut
O	Ne-ahs-jah	Owl
P	Bi-sodih	Pig
Q	Ca-yeilth	Quiver
R	Gah	Rabbit
S	Dibeh	Sheep
T	Than-zie	Turkey
U	No-da-ih	Ute
V	A-keh-di-glini	Victor
W	Gloe-ih	Weasel
X	Al-an-as-dzoh	Cross
Y	Tsah-as-zih	Yucca
Z	Besh-do-gliz	Zinc

Highlights of the Code

Military Term	Navajo Pronunciation	English Translation
America	Ne-he-mah	Our Mother
Major General	So-na-kih	Two Stars
Torpedo Plane	Tas-chizzie	Swallow
Fighter Plane	Da-he-tih-hi	Hummingbird
Transport Plane	Astah	Eagle
Battleship	Lo-tso	Whale
Aircraft Carrier	Tsidi-ney-ye-hi	Bird Carrier
Submarine	Besh-lo	Iron fish
Mine Sweeper	Cha	Beaver
Destroyer	Ca-lo	Shark
Cruiser	Lo-tso-yazzie	Small whale
Tank	Chay-da-gahi	Tortoise
Grenade	Ni-ma-si	Potatoes
Bomb	A-ye-shi	Egg
Bulldozer	Dola-alth-whosh	Bull sleep
Route	Gah-bih-tkeen	Rabbit trail
Fortification	Ah-na-sozi	Cliff dwelling

The original code, invented in the summer of 1942, contained 236 terms. In 1945, it was expanded to more than 400 terms, all still committed to memory. As a safeguard, the expanded code included alternate words for many of the most common letters of the alphabet. For example, "A" could be either ant, apple, or ax.

About the Author and Illustrator

Sara Hoagland Hunter is a writer/producer living in Weston, Massachusetts. She first became interested in Native American history as a student at Dartmouth College, where she met the Native American friend who would introduce her to the topic of the Navajo code talkers. Since that time, she and Julia Miner, who was also a Dartmouth classmate, have had the privilege of several research trips to the Navajo Reservation to interview former code talkers. Sara has written for Jim Henson Productions, Warner Bros., and Nickelodeon. Her other children's books include *Miss Piggy's Night Out* (Viking/Puffin) and *Rondo's Stuff* (Simon and Schuster). Sara's husband, Andy, and their two children, John and Abigail, are her inspiration and support team.

Julia Miner, an architect, has always enjoyed painting, children's literature, and travel. Research for her first children's book, *The Shepherd's Song: The Twenty-third Psalm* (Dial Books for Young Readers), took her to the Greek Islands, where she was able sketch and photograph shepherds at their work. While finishing the illustrations for *The Shepherd's Song* she moved from her home in New England to the Southwest. Captivated by the dramatic landscape, light, and people, she began to do more painting, especially portraits and landscapes. Julia lives in Paradise Valley, Arizona, with her husband, John Caldwell, and their daughter, Louisa.